The Special Parcel

by Audrey Tarrant

THE MEDICI SOCIETY LTD
LONDON
1985

THE SPECIAL PARCEL

'Hooray!' cried Sebastian Hopskip as he jumped out of bed, 'it's the last day of school today.'

'Hooray, it's snowing!' squeaked his sister Susie, as she pulled back the curtains.

When they had put their coats on ready to go to school, Mrs Hopskip tucked scarves warmly round their necks.

'Now, no snowballing on the way to school,' she warned them, 'or else you will sit in wet clothes all day!'

Happily Susie and Sebastian hopped and skipped along the snow-covered paths.

The schoolroom was very cold.

'Oh dear, oh dear!' tutted Miss Mole, as she poked and rattled the stove, 'it will NOT light this morning.'

The little animals sat at their desks and shivered, and their teeth began to CH. . . CH. . . CH. . . . CHATTER.

Miss Mole pushed in more paper and more sticks, and lit another match. The paper flared, the sticks sizzled . . . . . . and then went out again.

'I think the chimney must be blocked,' sighed Miss Mole.

$$2 + \underline{2}$$
$$2 + 5$$
$$3 + 4$$
$$6 + 3$$

5

'Susie and I could climb up on to the roof and try to clear it with a broom, Miss Mole,' said Sebastian.

Miss Mole was worried, but she looked at all the shivering animals and said, 'Very well then, here is the broom. Please DO be careful!'

It had stopped snowing as Sebastian and Susie climbed up the drainpipe on to the roof, and poked the broom down the chimney. They twisted and turned the broom — and then it stuck. They could not push it down; they could not pull it up!

'Thank you both for trying,' said Miss Mole, 'but I think we shall have to get Mr Brushbunny, the sweep, to clear it. This means we cannot light the stove today and, as the room is much too cold without it, I am going to give you an extra day's holiday.'

Squeaking and shouting with joy, the animals rushed into the snow. They had snowball fights and built a big snowrabbit.

Honk HONK! Honk HONK!

Susie heard the hooter as she carefully shaped the snowrabbit's ear.

'That's Mr Posthaste's horn,' she said; 'he must be bringing somebody a parcel.'

Again and again they heard Honk HONK! Honk HONK!.

'It sounds as though he is in trouble,' said Sebastian, 'let's go and see.'

They ran down the track past their house, and found it blocked by a snowdrift.

Honk HONK! Honk HONK!

'He's the other side of the snowdrift,' said Sebastian. 'Come on!'

Mr Posthaste, the hare, was very glad to see them.

'I have a special parcel for Mr Stripes-Black, the badger, marked FRAGILE. VERY URGENT,' he told them. 'I was trying to clear the snow to make way for the van when I slipped and fell and hurt my foot.'

The little animals ran to fetch spades and brooms, and soon they had cleared a way for the van. They swung the starting handle, but the engine only coughed and spluttered. They all pushed, but still it would not start.

'It's being awkward and WON'T go!' groaned Mr Posthaste.

Susie and Sebastian helped Mr Posthaste to hobble into their house, where Mrs Hopskip bandaged his foot.

'I MUST deliver that urgent parcel,' he said, 'I'll just have to walk.'

'Not with that foot you can't,' replied Mrs Hopskip.

'We can take it on our toboggan,' cried Susie. 'We can take the short-cut over Warren Hill, and then we'll be as quick as your van!'

Carefully they tied the parcel to the toboggan, and off they went. PULL. . . . Puff! PULL . . . . Puff! Up to the top of Warren Hill.

15

'Done it!' puffed Susie, as they stopped for breath at the top of the steep hill.

'It's lucky it's a big toboggan,' said Sebastian, 'there's room for us as well as the parcel. Come on. . . . now OFF we go!'

Whoosh   WHOOSH   WHOOSH! Down they flew!

'Mind those rabbits sliding at the bottom of the hill,' shrieked Susie in Sebastian's ear, as she clutched him tightly round the waist.

Faster and faster the toboggan whizzed down the hill.

'LOOK OUT!' yelled Sebastian.

'JUMP FOR IT,' shouted a rabbit, as the toboggan rushed down towards them. Susie and Sebastian put out their feet to stop the toboggan, but the rabbits' slide was so slippery that the toboggan would not stop – it raced straight towards THE POND!

SWOOOOSH!

Over the edge, on to the ice and across the pond it skated.

Susie and Sebastian WERE frightened!

In front of them they could see the ice was thinner, and near the bank it was broken.

'We MUST save the parcel,' thought Sebastian. 'It's fragile and it MUSTN'T fall in the water.'

'Put your left foot down HARD!' he shouted, and as they both put their left feet down, the toboggan turned on to the safe thicker ice. But it turned so quickly that Susie and Sebastian were thrown into the air and . . . . . .

SPLASH! They were gasping in the cold water.

'Hold on, we're coming,' they heard somebody shout, as they hung on to the reeds.

A family of water voles scurried down the bank, holding a ladder and ropes. They put the ladder across the ice, and one of the voles trod carefully across it. He tossed the ropes to Susie and Sebastian, and then, with a Heave HEAVE, the two squirrels were pulled safely on to the bank.

The water voles wanted Susie and Sebastian to come into their house and dry their clothes.

'C . . . can't stop, v . . very urgent p . . parcel,' said Sebastian with chattering teeth, 'n . . not far to g . . go.'

'Th . . thank you for s . . saving us,' said Susie, as the water voles pulled the toboggan up the bank for them.

They ran quickly along the path into the wood, past the hollow oak into Sett Place, and there was Mr Stripes-Black's front door.

Susie knocked loudly. RAT - A - TAT - TAT.

'Special delivery of your urgent parcel,' said Sebastian as Mr Stripes-Black opened the door.

'Thank you!' he said, then looked closely at them.

'Bless my whiskers! You're soaking wet, the pair of you! Come in and tell us about it.

Mrs Stripes-Black wrapped Susie and Sebastian in blankets and sat them in front of the fire while their clothes dried. She gave them hot drinks and toasted acorn sandwiches.

'Now you shall see what is in this VERY URGENT parcel,' said Mr Stripes-Black as he unwrapped it.

FAIRY LIGHTS AND CHRISTMAS TREE ORNAMENTS!

'We're having a Christmas party here for everyone,' said Mr Stripes-Black.

So on Christmas Day, there was a huge bonfire, chestnut soup and baked potatoes. They gathered round the Christmas tree with its bright lights and ornaments, sang carols and gave each other presents.

Mr Posthaste had a surprise present for Susie and Sebastian – caps with 'POSTHASTE PARCELS' on them.

'I need two small helpers to come with me in
my van, and sound my horn for me. Could
you help me in the school holidays?'

'OH, YES PLEASE!' squeaked Susie
and Sebastian. 'Honk HONK, Honk
HONK!'

© The Medici Society Ltd., London, 1985.
Printed in England.   B5 ISBN 0 85503 081